Original Korean text by Soo-bok Choi
Illustrations by Wal-goong Jang
Korean edition © Dawoolim

This English edition published by big & SMALL in 2016
by arrangement with Dawoolim
English text edited by Joy Cowley
English edition © big & SMALL 2016

Distributed in the United States and Canada by
Lerner Publishing Group, Inc.
241 First Avenue North
Minneapolis, MN 55401 U.S.A.
www.lernerbooks.com

ISBN: 978-1-925247-43-5

Printed in Korea

THE JOURNEY OF SEEDS

Written by Soo-bok Choi
Illustrated by Wal-goong Jang
Edited by Joy Cowley

big & SMALL

Seeds come in all shapes and sizes.
They do not move.
They are not magic.
So how do they make plants?

Coconut seed

Wisteria seeds

Viola seeds

Whitlow grass seeds

Flowers all bear seeds.

Sunflower seeds

Pomegranate seeds

Rice seeds

Some flowers are as small as fingernails.
Some flowers are as big as hands.
But they all bear seeds
after the flowers fall off.

Kidney bean seeds

Cosmos seeds

Apple seeds

Seeds are hiding inside the fruit.

Some fruits are small.
Some fruits are big.
The flesh of the fruit
covers the seeds inside.

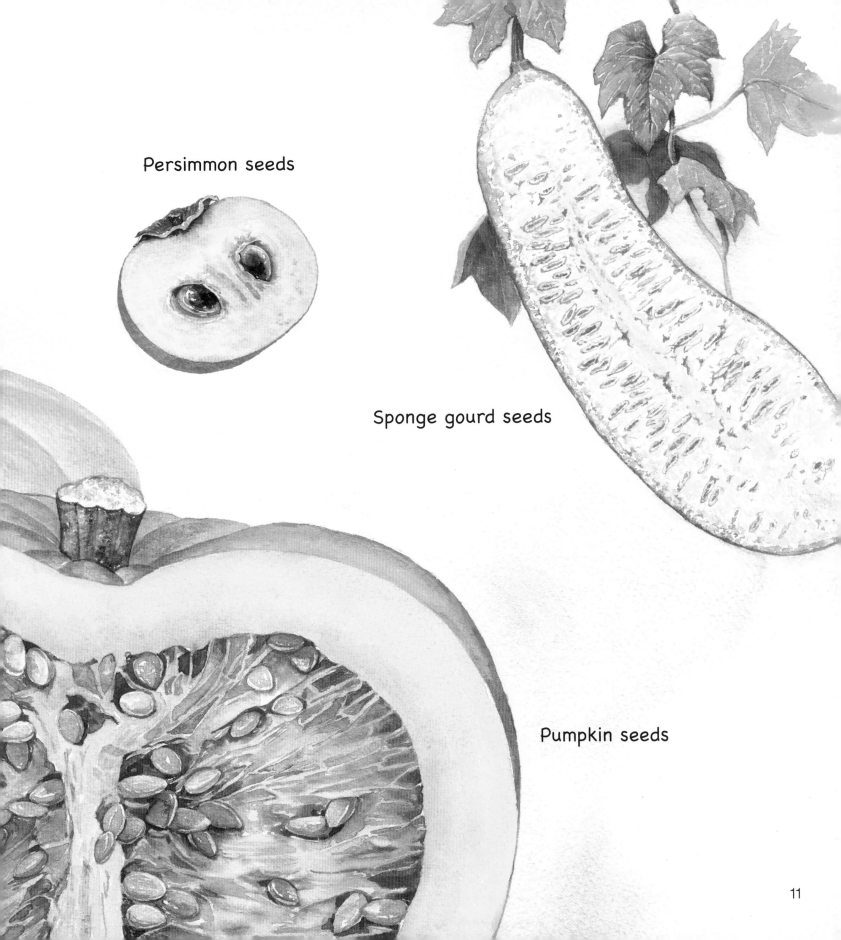

Persimmon seeds

Sponge gourd seeds

Pumpkin seeds

11

Yew seeds

Some seeds are on the outside.

Cycad seeds

pine nuts (seeds)

Some trees have needle-like leaves
that are green through winter.
Their seeds hang outside their fruits.

Maple seeds

The wind spreads these seeds.

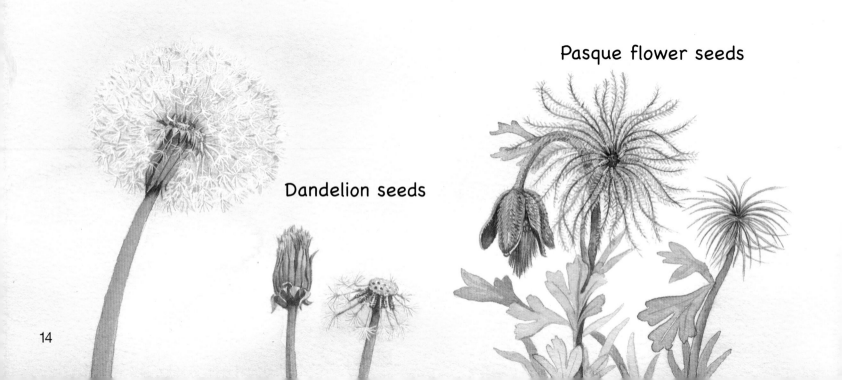

Pasque flower seeds

Dandelion seeds

There are seeds as light as cotton candy,
and seeds with wings.
They are waiting for the wind.

Where will they go?

White forsythia seeds

Seeds fly away to find new land.

Pasque flower seeds float like feathers.

Dandelion seeds drift like parachutes.

White forsythia seeds whirl like fans.

Maple seeds spin away on wings.

Black-jack seeds

Animals help the seeds spread.

Muscadine berries

Wild rose fruits

A bird eats red fruits and flies away.
Prickly seeds stick to a rabbit's fur.

Where do seeds go?

Cocklebur seeds

The bird drops dung.
The dung has lots of seeds in it.

The raccoon's dung
also has lots of seeds.

Seeds fall off animals.

The rabbit shakes its body
and the seeds come off.

The puppy scratches itself.
The seeds fall to the ground.

Water lily seeds

Morning glory seeds

Garden balsam seeds

Some plants spread their own seeds.

The seeds of morning glory
and the seeds of garden balsam
spring out from their pods.
Water lily seeds and coconut seeds
float on water.

Will the seeds sprout and grow?

Coconut seeds

Some seeds land on rock
and dry up in the sun.
Some are eaten by ants.
Some land in a spider's web.

24

But some seeds find good earth.
They sleep through winter,
waiting for spring.

With sunlight, water and rich earth,
the seeds wake up and send out
roots and a stem with leaves.

A new plant!

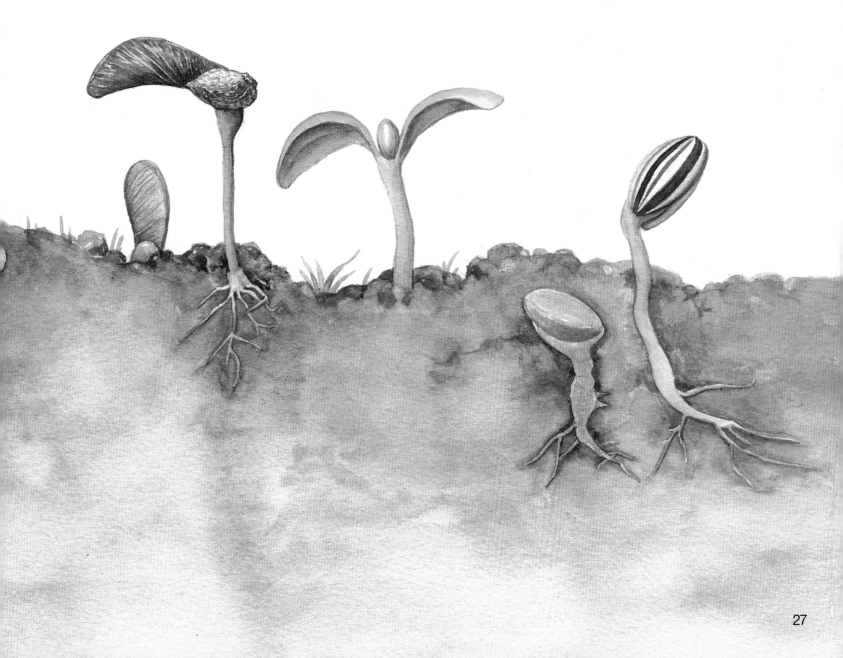

Seeds grow into plants.
Plants have flowers
and flowers produce
more seeds.

The Journey of Seeds

A seed contains a new life of the plant it will be.
Some seeds fly in the wind, some spring directly
from the plant, some travel with the help of animals.
When the seed finds good soil, it will grow as a new plant.

Let's think!

Do all plants have seeds?

Can you eat seeds?

How can the seeds in an apple become an apple tree?

How long can a seed survive without growing into a plant?

Let's do!

Imagine you are a seed and write a story about your journey
from the parent plant where you were made
to becoming a new plant yourself.

- What type of seed are you?

- How do you travel?

- How long does the journey take?